For R. Scott Mitchell
— M.B.

For Franklin Street Public School
— J.K.

ISBN 978-1-338-67384-5
10 9 8 7 6 5 4 3 2 1   22 23 24 25 26
Printed in China 62 · First edition, October 2022
Jon Klassen's illustrations were created with inks, watercolor, and graphite and compiled digitally. The text type and display type were set in Cheltenham ITC Std. The book was printed and bound by Leo Paper. Production was overseen by Catherine Weening. Manufacturing was supervised by Shannon Rice. The book was art directed by Patti Ann Harris, designed by Doan Buu, and edited by Andy Lopez Soberano and Liza Baker.

THE
THREE
BILLY GOATS GRUFF

Retold by MAC BARNETT

Illustrated by JON KLASSEN

Orchard Books
an Imprint of Scholastic Inc.
New York

Once upon a time,

there was a bridge.

And beneath that bridge,

there lived a troll.

The troll would sit in the mud

and the rubble and trash,

listening,

waiting,

hoping for someone to cross

the bridge above his head.

"I am a troll. I live to eat.

I love the sound of hooves and feet

and paws and claws on cobblestones.

For that's the sound of meat and bones!"

The troll used a filthy fingernail
to scrape the wax out of his ears.

All he'd eaten lately was a leather boot
and some goop he'd found in his belly button.

He was practically starving.

"Clip, clop! Clip, clop!"

went the bridge above his head.

The troll scrambled to his feet

and climbed into the light, crying,

"Who seeks to reach the grassy ridge?

Who dares to walk across my bridge?"

A little goat stood there, quivering.

"It's only me," said the goat.

"A billy goat. My last name's Gruff."

The troll began to dance and stomp.

"I *love* goat! Let me count the ways.

A rump of goat in honey glaze.

Goat smoked, goat poached, a goat pot roast.

Goat smorgasbord! Goat smeared on toast!

A goat kale salad — hold the kale.

Goat escargot! (That's goat plus snails.)

On goat I'll dine, on goat I'll sup.

You little goat, I'll eat you up!"

"Please!" said the little goat. "No!

You don't want to eat me!

There's hardly any meat on my bones!"

The troll squinted.

Now that he mentioned it,

this goat did look kind of stringy.

The little goat smiled.

"If you let me cross, I'll tell you a secret:

Soon my big brother will come this way,

and he is much fatter and tastier than I am."

"Your big brother, huh?" said the troll.

He tugged the long hair that grew from his chin.

"OK. You may pass."

And the first Billy Goat Gruff trotted
clip clop clip clop across the bridge.

Down below, the troll chuckled to himself.

"I can't believe I tricked that goat

into telling me about his big brother.

I'm so smart!

And fun and handsome."

"Clip, clop! Clip, clop!" went the bridge
above his head.

The troll scrambled to his feet
and climbed into the light, crying,

"Who seeks to reach the grassy ridge?
Who dares to walk across my bridge?"

It was another goat.

"It's only me," said the goat.

"The second of the Billy Goats Gruff."

The troll was glad to see this goat was not so small.
He clapped his hands together and squealed.

"I *love* goat! Let me count the ways!

Goat Benedict with hollandaise.

Goat jerky, jerk goat, curried goat.

Goat gravy in a silver boat.

A goat flambé with candied yams.

A goat clambake, with goat, not clams!

On goat I'll dine, on goat I'll sup.

You little goat, I'll eat you up!"

"Please!" said the goat. "No!
You don't want to eat me."

The troll frowned.
"Why not? You look delicious."

The second goat smiled.

"I would only spoil your appetite.

For if you let me cross, I'll tell you a secret:

Soon my big brother will come this way,

and he is much fatter and tastier than I am."

"*Your* big brother, huh?"

The troll whistled.

"I'd sure like to see that."

He twirled his chin hair around his finger.

"OK. You may pass."

And the second Billy Goat Gruff trotted
clip clop clip clop across the bridge.

Crouching down there in the dark,

the troll was bursting with anticipation.

"This third brother sounds positively mouthwatering!

I can't wait to eat him."

The troll picked at a scab.

"What rhymes with strudel?"

"CLIP, CLOP! CLIP, CLOP!" went the bridge.

The troll began drooling.

"Oh my.

Here we go!"

He scrambled to his feet

and flung himself into the light, crying,

"Who seeks to reach the grassy ridge?

Who dares to walk across my bridge?"

"Oh . . ." said the troll. "Um . . .

I, uh . . .

I . . .

Wow. You're really big."

The troll straightened himself up as tall
as he could, coughed, and said
in a voice that sounded quite small,
"I'll eat you up . . . you little goat."

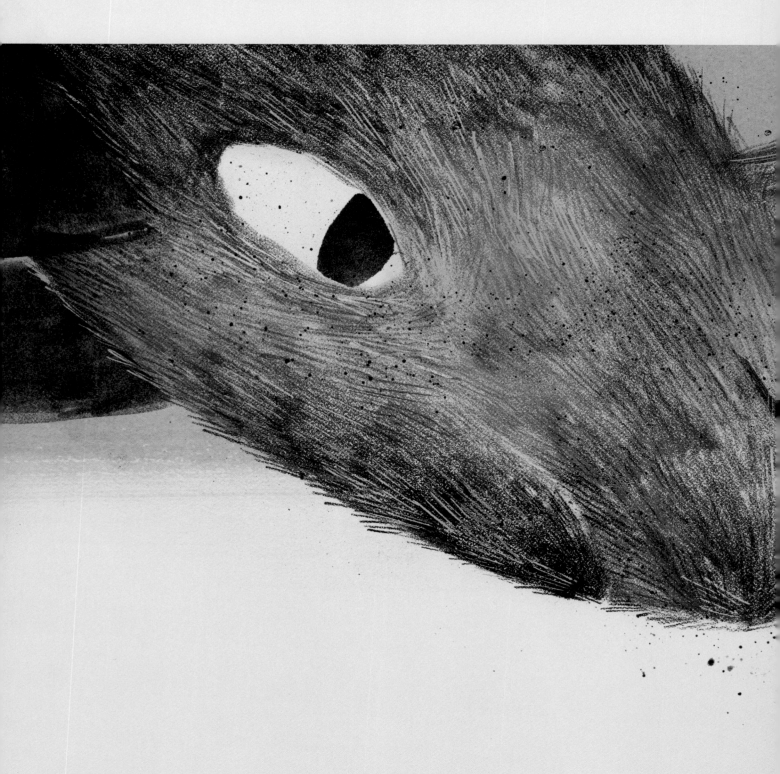

The big goat laughed.

He lowered his horns

and stamped his hoof.

"No," said the goat. "You will not."

And the third Billy Goat Gruff

rammed into the troll,

who flew off the bridge,

into the rapids,

and over the waterfall

which was known as

"The Big Waterfall."

Then he went over

"The Huge Waterfall."

And
then
came
the
waterfall
we
call
"The
Really
Enormous
Waterfall."

The troll floated down the river,

around the bend.

Where he ended up, I really can't say.

I've never gone that far.

There are too many mosquitoes.

As for the third goat,

he trotted clip clop clip clop

and joined his brothers on the grassy ridge.

The three Billy Goats Gruff are still there today,

eating all they want, getting nice and fat.

You can go visit them and say hello.

All you have to do

is cross the bridge.